The Magic Toolbox

Starring Fred and Lulu

Mie Araki

chronicle books · san francisco

On Monday, Lulu built a boat.

Fred built a house, but it fell down.

"Too bad," said Lulu.

"Phooey!" said Fred.

On Tuesday, Lulu built a dragon.
Fred built a house, but it fell down.

"What a shame," said Lulu.

"Nuts!" said Fred.

On Wednesday, Lulu built a train.
Fred built a house,
but it fell down.

"You'll do better when you're bigger," said Lulu.

"I give up!" said Fred, and he went outside to swing.

"I'll never be able to build a house,"
Fred mumbled.

To his surprise, somebody answered.
A strange box had appeared beneath the tree.
It was a magic toolbox.

"With me at your side,
you can build anything," it said.

square

brush

T-square

pencil

paintbrush

ruler

eraser

paper

paint

roller

snacks

tape

"I want to build a house,"
said Fred.

"Dandy," said the toolbox,
and it tossed its tools
out on the lawn.

saw

hinges

nails & screws

hammer

trowel

wrench

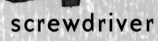

screwdriver

tape measure

pliers

goggles

Band-Aids

ladder

With the paper and pencil,
Fred designed a house.

"This is difficult," he said.

"Have a cherry lollipop," said the toolbox.

Fred measured and sawed the lumber.
"I can do it!" he said.

"Oh, you can, you can," said the toolbox.

And hammered—
"Oops!"

"I have plenty
of Band-Aids,"
said the toolbox.

Fred laid the bricks for the chimney.
"Wait till Lulu sees this!" he said.

He hung the door on its hinges.
"Lulu will never believe this!"

Finally Fred painted his house.
"Eat your heart out, Lulu," he said.
"Here she comes," said the toolbox
as it juggled the paint cans.

Lulu was astonished.

"That is some house!" she said.
"How did you do it?"

"Nothing to it," said Fred,
"when you have the right tools."

5/03

**To Stan
and Sky**

Book design by Kristen M. Nobles.
Typeset in Ad Lib and BaseNine.

The illustrations in this book were carved
in birch plywood and printed in watercolor paint
on Japanese rice paper.

Manufactured in Hong Kong.

Band-Aid is a trademark of the
Johnson & Johnson Consumer Products Company.

Library of Congress Cataloging-in-Publication Data
Araki, Mie.
The magic toolbox: starring Fred and Lulu / by Mie Araki.
p. cm.
Summary: Lulu the rhinoceros is good at building things and once
Fred the rabbit finds a magic toolbox, he can build things too.
ISBN 0-8118-3564-2
[1. Building-Fiction. 2. Magic-Fiction. 3. Toolboxes-Fiction.
4. Tools-Fiction. 5. Rabbits-Fiction. 6. Rhinoceroses-Fiction.]
I. Title.
PZ7.A663 Fr 2003
[E]--dc21
2002004468

Distributed in Canada by Raincoast Books
9050 Shaughnessy Street
Vancouver, British Columbia V6P 6E5

10 9 8 7 6 5 4 3 2 1

Chronicle Books LLC
85 Second Street
San Francisco, California 94105

www.chroniclekids.com